ISLAND CHRISTMAS

Callie Browning

Also by Callie Browning

The Girl with the Hazel Eyes

The Vanishing Girls

The Secrets of Catspraddle Village

Collaborative Works

The Midnight Hour Anthology

Copyright

Island Christmas
Copyright 2024 © by Callie Browning
ISBN: 978-976-8306-13-5

All rights reserved under International and Pan-American Copyright Conventions.

By payment of the required fees, you have been granted the nonexclusive, nontransferable right to access and read the text of this book. No part of this text may be reproduced, decompiled, transmitted, downloaded, reverse-engineered or stored in or introduced into any information storage and retrieval system in any form or by any means, whether electronic or mechanical, now known or hereafter invented, without the express permission of the author, her estate or duly appointed agents.

With the exception of quotes used in reviews, this book may not be reproduced in whole or in part by any means existing without written permission from the author.

FIRST EDITION

This is a work of fiction. Names, characters, places and incidents either are the product of the author's imagination or are used fictiously. Any resemblance to actual persons, living or dead, and some events is entirely coincidental.

Trigger Warning

War

Chapter 1

8th December, 1941

Barbados

Annie shielded her eyes and squinted at the newspaper stand across the busy Bridgetown street. It was the 826th day of battle but it felt twice as long since the war had started. And yesterday the Japanese dragged America into it, pummeling Pearl Harbour with their fleet carriers and aircraft. The attack had easily motivated the Americans to join a war they had fought tooth and nail to avoid. Before the smoke had cleared, America's President Roosevelt had entered the fray.

The idea of it spreading had been an abstract concept until Germany invaded Poland. Then, just like a schoolyard skirmish, most of Europe jumped in to defend Poland and it trickled down to the colonies. What Caribbean people thought was a mere disagreement between a few countries in far-flung places now dictated every aspect of their lives from what they ate to being fined or imprisoned for lighting lanterns. Barbadians were already tired. Another conflict so soon after the Great War, the Great Depression and the 1937 riots in Bridgetown. The misery of it was impossible to escape. Photos of bombed buildings and ration notices took up more and more space in the broadsheets and on the wires, filtering down into talk at the taverns and rum shops. Throw in the blackouts and propaganda posters and war was more effective than a guilty conscience at keeping you up at night.

  While Japan was bombing America, Annie was home darning bedsheets for Mrs. Hawkins, the mean little woman in the great house at the centre of the village. Old lady Hawkins gave her ten pence and six eggs from the yard fowls she kept around back. Annie generally had trouble keeping her face neutral in the face of foolishness but the war worked better than farm grade tranquilisers to immobilise muscles that would otherwise sneer at such meagre pay. Things were hard but the family found ways to stretch money. Ma sold mauby to field workers. Annie took any work she could to help make up the rest. Gracie, seventeen, looked after the house, handling the cooking, washing and whatever else needed to be done. Fourteen year old Wilbert was still in school but had started 'refurbishing coupon books' as he called it. He'd rigged up some old equipment he'd found at an abandoned printery and kept stashed behind the pit toilet house. Ma used the counterfeit books but judiciously, her Christianity at odds with making her children starve. Just before she'd left home, Annie warned him again that it was illegal but Wilbert didn't seem to care.

The wind picked up and leaves scuttled across Trafalgar Square into the Careenage. Annie pressed her hat on her head, bustling past the pier-side bay office where a line of weary travellers waited to get their permits stamped. Overhead, fluffy clouds dotted the blue sky as boats bobbed gently on the water. Dockhands scurried along moving cargo and luggage as the last few passengers disembarked from the small lighters that ferried people and possessions from the big ships to the shore.

Most men didn't stick out to her but he did. He made himself stick out even more by walking a few steps behind her and casually whistling a big band melody. Annie kept moving, impulsively tightening her grip on her handbag because she'd left her ration book inside. Two days earlier, a neighbour told Annie that a street urchin had snatched her sister's ration book and shopping bag from her shoulder before darting down a narrow dirt path. "Thieves want coupons," she'd advised with a knowing nod of her grey head as she smacked her lips. "These days I does wrap the ration book inside my string bags, clutch them tight inside my purse and go to the market."

Behind Annie the man kept tune, his whistling clean and clear like bird song. Then he said in a voice more refined than white sugar, "Good morning, miss. Would you like to make some extra money?"

Annie stopped short, intent on telling this man exactly what he could do with his suppositions about her when he grinned, clearly amused with his own irreverence. He clarified with a twinkle in his eye, "I'd be more than willing to pay you to direct me to a good boarding-house. Some place parasite-free and close to the docks. I'm as fond of long commutes as I am to ticks and lice, thus my specificity."

She looked him up and down. For all of his polish, there was a roguish air to him: his suitcase was clearly expensive, but his hat was cocked to a side, his chin was making a valiant attempt to sprout a beard and his tie was firmly askew as though he'd purposely fixed it that way.

"With the amount of sailors and travellers knocking around the country at this time of the year, only the old Sheriff's Lodge might be a good fit for you. It's called Seaview, I believe. No payment necessary."

"Where's that?" he asked falling in step beside Annie.

"About a kilometre up the road from here. After the Garrison, just at the top of the hill that goes down to Grave's End."

He quirked his brow. "The hotel is next to a cemetery? Doesn't sound as upscale as you'd have me believe."

Annie laughed, relaxing her grip on her handbag as she looked up at him. "Grave's End is a beach." A mischievous grin lit her eyes. "The cemetery is on the *other* side of it."

"Oh my…a curious place is Little England, isn't it?"

She smiled, taking her time to wait as two men on bicycles wheeled past before she crossed the road. "The hotel is ideally situated if you ask me; next to a beach, quiet neighbours."

His shrug was good-natured, acquiescent. "Touché. Where are you off to, if I might ask?"

"To a meeting in Bridgetown." She glanced at him. "In the *opposite* direction to Seaview, I might add."

"What's a brisk jaunt in the hot sun between friends?"

"Friends?"

"Alexander James, engineer and friend extraordinaire. Alex for short. Pleased to make your acquaintance." He slowed his pace, holding out his hand to Annie who stopped walking and offered hers in return.

"Anastasia Jones, street concierge. But everyone calls me Annie."

And right there, in the shade of Lord Nelson's statue, Alexander James gently rotated her hand, bringing a subtle arch to her wrist as he lifted it to his lips and kissed it.

"The world is at war, not you and I," he murmured, casting hooded eyes up at Annie. "You're disarming but unarmed so I already know you bore no ill will toward me."

Annie's heart stuttered and her lips didn't know how to behave as they tried to form words. In the end, all she could get out was a breathy, "Pardon?"

"That's where the custom of handshakes comes from. To let your enemies see that you aren't hiding any weapons."

"Oh…" She hated how dim and slow she sounded. 'Foolishy-foolishy' as her grandmother would say.

"Plus… I'd rather tell myself I got to kiss you on our first meeting. I am a man, after all," Alex said with a sly grin as he slowly released her hand.

Good heavens, isn't he though? The very epitome of man with impossibly smooth skin, angular features and dreamy brown eyes. Annie tried not to sigh, but her emotions surged through her with such intensity that they could only leave her body via a slow gust of air through her mouth.

"Yes," was all she could reply. She nodded dimly and began walking again, forcing herself to change the subject. "So… where did you sail in from?"

"Great Britain."

"Ah…trying to get away from the cold?"

"Not so much. I live here. It was time to come back."

"What sent you to Big England?"

He smirked, amused by her remembrance of him calling Barbados Little England. He cocked his shoulder. "Eh…you know. Sight-seeing. Tea-drinking. This-ing and that-ing."

"The life of Riley."

"Or so I'd make you believe," Alex said with an easy smile. "But only if sight-seeing happens as I belly-crawl across frozen fields or tea-drinking means scarfing down rations that impersonate food on a very imaginative level."

Annie eyed him again and grinned at his confirmation that his laissez-faire look was intentional. "So you're a soldier then?"

"Am I that obvious?"

Annie smiled. "Perhaps…but whether you are or not will have to remain unseen. We've reached my destination."

Alex looked up at the two-story building sandwiched between other similar structures, its wide wooden gallery bearing a sign proclaiming it to be "The Spice House".

"All good things do come to an end, don't they? Are you sure I can't pay you for your help?"

"Quite sure. It was nice meeting you, Mr. James. I hope you enjoy your walk to the hotel." Annie smiled and offered her hand again, her cheeks warming as Alex pressed a gentle kiss against her folded fingers.

"I will." With a tip of his hat and an easy smile, Alex turned on his heel and headed back up the road.

Annie watched him walk away, her heart sagging a little beneath her disappointment. Alex was tall and funny and charming. And his eyes. Sigh. Penetrating, smouldering and warm all at once. Whoever had engineered Alex had done yeoman duty to womankind. Annie had been wary of him at first but she'd sensed something building between them. But then he left without asking where she lived so he could call on her or send a letter. She would have asked how she could contact him but her pride wouldn't let her. Plus she couldn't be late for her job interview.

Chapter 2

Annie turned by the cannon embedded in the wall on her right, her brown leather heels clicking against the stone as she walked. Sunlight was muted between the buildings, a perfect place for moss to thrive on the bricked alleyway and for small ferns to sprout from the cracks in the wall. She found the doorway halfway down the alley as instructed and went in, climbing the varnished stairs on the left to the second floor. Annie knocked on the door at the top of the landing and heard a sharp voice say, "Come!" the moment her hand left the wood's smooth surface.

The room was generic with its mahogany panelling, stained desk, caned chairs and artless walls, save for the sharply dressed white man smoking up the room with an overpriced cigar. His grey hair was neatly cut and round glasses framed his no-nonsense blue eyes. He glanced up at Annie, brandishing a pen toward the vacant chair on the other side of his desk as he read documents in front of him.

"Good morning," Annie said as she took her seat.

"Morning, morning," the man replied, never looking up from the papers. Even upside down Annie could see her name and address written on the file. "I'm Frank Bastion. And you're Anastacia Jones of Hawthorn Village, St. Michael, correct?"

"Yes," Annie said hesitantly. "Mr. Bastion, I understood from the letter I got that I was being interviewed for a job... but I'm a bit embarrassed to admit that while I am looking for work, I don't recall asking for a job that might have led me here to you."

Frank shifted the papers. "And?"

Annie chuckled nervously. "Well...I went to the telephone exchange on Bay Street and the dry goods store in Trafalgar Square. Neither had vacancies...but I didn't leave my information with them either."

"Uh huh?"

Annie cleared her throat and twisted her fingers in her lap. She knew not to look a gift horse in the mouth but she also believed that anything that was too good to be true probably was.

Frank finally looked up at her and said, "You've been conscripted, Miss Jones," in the same tone one uses to explain that rain's coming. "We need a new clerk at one of our offices and your experience as a typist makes you ideally suited for the job."

Annie raised an eyebrow. "Conscripted? But I thought they didn't want …"

She hesitated, catching Frank's blue eyes as he waited for her to finish speaking. "…some people in the war effort."

"That's changing. Our orders are to recruit as many good men — and women — as we can, no matter their colour. By next year we'll have a West Indian group in the Auxiliary Transport Service in Great Britain, which is the women's branch of the army."

Annie nodded, her heart thudding. Clerical work meant a steady pay cheque. A steady *government* pay cheque at that. Far away from the frontlines and in good weather. All she had to do was stick out the war, save her money and get to Switzerland to start afresh. She was bored here and tired of the lack of opportunities. And it shouldn't be much longer now given that it had been almost three years since the war started. But...

"Did you say 'next year'?"

Frank raised an eyebrow, unamused. "I did. You can type and file, right?"

"Uh, yes, twenty words a minute. But the papers said the war won't go on much longer since the Americans are in it now. And that..."

Frank waggled his cigar so hard a thick stub of ash flew off and landed on the floor.

"First thing: stop reading the broadsheets. Listen to what *we* tell you." He picked up a pen, made a slight tick on the page in front of him and asked, "What about franking and sending telegraphs?"

Absolutely no manners, Annie thought as she pursed her mouth into a tight pink circle. *My grandmother would cut this man's ass 'til he turned blue.* "Yes, I can do both of those. How else will we know what's going on?"

Frank shook his head not unlike a teacher at a dunce who asked to leave early. "Do you really think the Ministry of Defence is so *dim* as to plaster its deepest darkest secrets in the news to help Hitler plan his next move? What isn't sanitised is made up when it comes to the cause so don't get too muddled about it."

Frank pulled a stamp from his desk and poised it over the paper. Almost as an afterthought, he glanced at Annie and asked gruffly, "Any questions?"

Annie hmphed to herself. "No, Mr. Bastion. None at all."

The stamp came down with a bang, inking a black circle with the word "RECRUITED" next to her name.

"Report to the white building on Humpton Street tomorrow at 0700 hours for training. The officer on duty will direct you from there," Frank said, handing her the paper and an envelope. "Happy to have you on board."

Well, Annie thought as she bid him goodbye and left the room, *at least he didn't try to look down my blouse.* If there was one thing she was good at, it was finding a silver lining.

***

No sooner than Annie's footsteps had receded down the stairs did a knock sound on the door behind Frank's desk. "Come," Frank said, his voice much lower this time. The door opened and closed and Alex slid smoothly into the chair Annie had just vacated. He'd adjusted his tie so that it now sat neatly at the apex of his collar, fixed his hat and somehow straightened his posture all in time for his audience with Frank.

"So?" Frank mumbled around his cigar.

"She's sharp, gregarious. Talks a lot but doesn't say much. Not eager for money. Or at least small amounts of it," Alex reported.

"We all have a price, it's true," Frank agreed as he stubbed out his cigar.

"But why her?"

"She was one of those trouble makers during the '37 riots. Police didn't catch her, but our people took note. Since then she had a job with a chemist typing labels and order forms so she's probably pretty accurate when it comes to the secretarial bit. Chemist closed last year; owner died with no heirs. Plus, her brother is a forger. Petty stuff for now but it doesn't take much to tip the scales in times like these. Best to keep her close."

"So she's good at evasion?"

Frank's blue gaze pensive as he looked at Alex. "I guess we'll see. Get started. See how she does."

"Will do."

Frank cleared his throat and tapped his fingers on the desk. "There's uh…just one quick note I've been told to make."

Alex raised an eyebrow. Frank was a career military man. Whatever was making him nervous must be important.

"Since this is the first time we're integrating female troops, fraternisation rules are being strictly enforced. Even though the two of you won't face combat together, a small unit such as one on a Caribbean island means close quarters."

Alex met his gaze squarely. "Noted."

"And given the sensitive nature of information received by our section, spies are particularly forbidden to engage in…" He glanced up at Alex, his face pinched at the fact that he'd been tasked with a chore he considered beneath him. "…familiar relations. I run a tight ship and don't want my section called into question. So keep your little soldier away from her. Understood?"

With a straight face, Alex gave a curt nod and left the room.

Chapter 3
9th December, 1941

If Annie hadn't been looking for the building she would have walked straight past. Peeling paint on its façade, rebellious weeds poking their way through pebbled marl that had long ago lost its snow-white brilliance and no signage whatsoever. *Which makes sense*, Annie realised as she knocked on the door. Footsteps sounded from within and when the door opened, Annie was only half surprised to see the man she'd met yesterday standing before her. A broad smile lit her face.

"Good morning, Mr. James," Annie said with a nod of her head as she stepped inside. "If that is your real name."

Alex chuckled. "Why wouldn't it be? This way." He pointed to the back of the building and led the way through the corridor.

"Why *would* it be? Last night it dawned on me that our meeting wasn't by chance. Once I realised what my job interview was about I figured you were probably a one-man advance team."

Alex peered at her over his shoulder, his eyes searching hers. His face was impassive but Annie sensed a smile hidden in his eyes. "Chance is the world's way of showing us what's possible."

Annie followed in his wake, her cheeks warm and her eyes roving the open spaces they walked by. The front room was just as devoid of character as the outside of the building save for the Union Jack and a smattering of vintage maps on the wall. The small storage nook under the staircase was packed to the brim with dusty boxes. At the end of the corridor was a large file cabinet and a single desk where the remains of Alex's breakfast was attracting flies. He opened the door to a room with a typewriter and a stack of paper neatly arranged on a desk.

Alex gestured to the desk and Annie sat in the chair. He took that 'at ease' stance soldiers do and said, "You've got 10 minutes to produce a report of your time in this building."

Annie stared at Alex. "But…I just got here."

"Exactly. I'll be back in 10 minutes."

***

Alex pulled the door closed and shook his head irritably. Try as he might, disguising his attraction to Annie was harder than it needed to be. He'd worried that Frank would notice when he'd given his initial assessment of her. Alex practically felt his interest in her radiating off of him in waves. She was sharper than he realised and every time he looked at her it was like being yanked forward by an invisible tether. A part of him hoped she'd fail the first test because then he could pursue a relationship with her. The other part of him would hate for that to happen. Smart, beautiful women were his Achilles heel, a treat for both his eyes and his mind. He'd kick himself if he'd misjudged her intellect.

Sliding into his chair and without thinking, Alex tapped his pen on the side of the desk, his mind wandering. If Annie failed the assessment they'd stick her in some random desk job to put her filing and typing skills to good use. If Annie did a good job, his orders were to start training her. Introductory stuff of course: weapons, interrogation, some hand-to-hand combat, surveillance and other things. This far away from the front, the top guys didn't imagine she'd need much more. The amount of spies on the island was limited at best; the only person he'd met was Frank but based on little things he'd seen and heard, he knew they weren't the only ones. Even so, he doubted the number even hit double digits. But at his level he didn't know very much anyway. And if Annie ever needed to be transferred out, they'd give her more training when she got wherever she was going. But Alex was getting ahead of himself. She needed to finish the test first. He snapped himself out of his reverie and opened the newspaper. Despite what Frank said, he still enjoyed reading the paper. To Alex's mind, knowing the truth and what the papers masqueraded as the truth were both important. A public lie has value and impacts the way the masses navigate their world. Underestimating or ignoring that was the bigger mistake to Alex's mind. But Alex was no fool; he suspected all of the top brass read the broadsheets religiously and told the rank and file spies not to read the news so they had greater control over them. That's what Alex would do.

Alex scanned the paper, slightly surprised by the number of Christmas ads he was seeing. "Oh yes, it's December," he muttered to himself. Between training and travel, it had slipped his mind that something as normal as Christmas could still exist. There were ads for marl so 'you and your family can have a white Christmas', sixty cent silk shirts for the boys and men of the house, fresh cassava for Christmas pone. He'd chosen his mother's gift since August, a pair of delicate sterling silver earrings from a luxury shop in London run by a man and his four sons who crafted every piece by hand. His father's gift was a watch fob he'd gotten off a bloke at the dock in Southhampton, no doubt the spoils of post-blitz looting. Alex had wrapped each gift in cloth, tied them with ribbon and stuck small notes beneath the folds just in case he was deployed or killed in combat and didn't make it back for Christmas. Finishing his shopping so early had put the entire thing out of his mind. Alex looked at his watch. Annie's time was almost up.

Just beyond the closed door behind him, the chair scraped the wooden floor, Annie's footsteps drew closer and the door opened with a slight creak. She walked to his desk and placed a neatly typed sheet of paper on it.

"Thank you," he said as he picked up the paper. "You can return to your seat and I'll review. Shouldn't take more than five minutes."

With a curt nod, she left the room.

It didn't take him long. All he read was:

First room:
3 maps - (1) Signal Station map. Beige with the island outlined in red and drawings of four signal stations. Dark brown frame. Noviffima et Acuratiffima BARBADOS descriptio Johannem Ogiluium, Cartographers.

(2) Map of Barbados. Off white with island outlined in dark blue, parishes outlined in red, towns noted in green. Commissioned by Lord Norman in 1897, cartographers Williams, Walker & Wade (Colonial Merit) 1899.

Alex scanned the paper in disbelief. She described the printed boxes under the staircase, the labels on the file cabinet… on and on she went for the entire page. All without a single typographical error. Less than a minute later Alex went into the room, his face perplexed, paper held aloft in his hand.

"You've got a photographic memory?"

"A what?"

Alex stared at her, mouth agape. "It means you see things once and it's stored in your head like a photograph."

Annie shrugged. "Doesn't everyone?"

He squinted at her. "If we did, there'd be no need for exams or re-reading books."

"I've always wondered about that," Annie admitted with a wrinkle of her pretty face.

Alex chuckled. This was better than either he or Frank could have hoped. He pulled up a chair across from her and observed her for a moment. She was watching him, her face a mixture of amusement and curiosity.

"You've done well, Miss Jones. From now on everything we do and everything you see is confidential. We'll start your training immediately."

Annie's eyes opened wide. "So there's more to my job than typing and filing?"

Alex smirked. "Much more."

Chapter 4

12th December, 1941

Many Bajans looked forward to December. Sun-scorched days abated to make way for slightly cooler weather, bringing with it vibrant changes to the island's landscape. Snow-on-the-mountain shrubs quietly blanched as the temperatures dipped, the plant's small green starbursts turning white. Poinsettias went from green to scarlet, going from supporting act to the star of many a humble garden. Children shrieked with joy as they caught tiny Christmas worms and took them inside to their parents as proof that the holiday season's glad tidings would soon be upon them. But it also meant that the rainy season was in full swing.

The sun had barely risen and it was still drizzling when Alex turned the car off Humpton Street and onto the open gravel area. Annie was already there in the middle of the small porch trying to escape the rain.

Cursing under his breath, Alex pulled up the brake and hustled out of the car. "Morning. So sorry, Annie. I didn't realise you'd be this early or I would have made sure you didn't have to stand outside."

"Good morning," Annie replied with a slight shiver as the wind changed direction and dusted her in rain drops. "I didn't realise either but I figured early is better than late."

"We'll make you a soldier yet with that kind of thinking," Alex grinned as he unlocked the door and let them inside. His face sobered. "But I truly am sorry. Of course, I could…"

Alex gripped his tongue between his teeth, catching himself before he could add "come to pick you up every morning." This was the problem with being attracted to his trainee. His conscience told him that everything he said would reek of impropriety and scream that he was interested in her. Last night he'd lain in bed thinking about her and cursed the operations people for not choosing a little old lady or someone less beautiful, less engaging to take up her post. Twelve hour days for the past three days in close confines had done nothing to expose any strange habits. Just the opposite. Alex found her even sexier and more beguiling. Now Annie watched him closely, tilting her head in his direction as she waited for him to finish his sentence.

"...make a point to be here by six to avoid it happening again."

"I appreciate that." Annie put her handbag on the wall hook and smoothed her skirt. She turned to Alex and looked at him expectantly.

"Sit. Please," he said, pulling out a chair for her before he mentally kicked himself. *She's your subordinate and a spy. Stop acting like you're courting her!*

"Right...so, today, we're going to work on evasion," Alex said, sitting on the other side of the desk. "Evasion is kind of broad but that's by design. It's necessary during conversations, if being followed and in lots of other situations." Alex turned a pen over in his hands as he held Annie's eyes with his. "What I'm about to show you is a double-edged sword because these are things you'll also need to learn to look for in other people so you can assess their frame of mind and their intentions."

"Alright," Annie nodded as she listened.

"It's natural for your family to want to know about your work. And it's natural for you to want to tell them about it. But given the nature of what we do, you may recall that you can't tell them anything."

Annie took a deep breath and nodded again.

"You could lie or say nothing. But always think about how they know you operate under normal circumstances and give them some variance of that. Anything too far off will make people suspicious and be harder to remember."

Alex stood and walked around the desk, pacing back and forth behind Annie as she stared at his now vacant chair.

"Emotions bleed. Like just now…when I told you that you can't tell your family. You held your breath. Which indicates stress. That tells me you're close to your family and the idea of lying to them doesn't fill you with ribbons of delight."

Annie giggled. "That's an interesting way to put it."

"And true. Don't forget that."

Annie looked up at him with a smile and it was all Alex could do not to lock eyes with her and suggest they spend the day at the beach getting to know each other instead. He turned away and said, "Cloak your emotions while watching every infinitesimal signal the other person gives you. Are they stressed? Happy? Too excited? Too wary? Of course, there are levels to emotions, things that the casual onlooker may not be able to glean without knowing the person or their history intimately. But anything outside of the normal range should arouse suspicion."

Alex tapped the back of her chair. "Stand and turn to me…"

Alex didn't think himself a cad by even the slightest degree. But this particular lesson would make him look like one if he wasn't careful. Upstairs, rain-washed wind whistled through the jalousie windows and down the stairs rustling a stack of papers on the desk behind them. Annie's soap or perfume — Alex wasn't sure which— filled his nostrils. Lavender and rose, or something of the sort. Getting through this lesson without exposing his emotions was going to require more concentration than he'd bargained for.

"Everyone has a band of personal space and when that's compromised it makes the average person very fidgety."

Alex took a breath and stepped closer. The floorboards flexed beneath his feet, creaking slightly. Now mere inches separated them. As expected, Annie's breathing was quick and she blinked too rapidly, but she kept her eyes straight ahead. Alex glanced down and immediately she stopped rubbing her fingertips. "Good," he said. "Little signals like nervous fingers give the other person cues that tell them how to respond to you."

"Sorry."

"It's natural. You'll become accustomed. You'll be in a clerical role but your ability to observe people will be crucial. You can't give them any sign that you're more than what you say you are."

"Okay," Annie bobbed her head in understanding before she exhaled and squared her shoulders.

"Steady yourself. Regulate your breathing. Clear your mind."

She did as she was told and gradually her breathing grew calm, her body relaxed.

"Separate yourself from your reality. Never avert your eyes but don't stare. Now, try it with me."

"Try what?"

"Look at me."

The rise and fall of her chest that was so calm just a few seconds earlier quickened. Annie took another deep breath and for a moment she continued to stare straight ahead. Slowly, without moving her head, she tilted her eyes upward until coffee coloured eyes met cocoa coloured eyes. They were soft at first, gentled by something that she didn't say and Alex didn't dare ask. That look arrested him, inflated his heart and made it thud against his chest despite his best intentions. He felt that tether again, that irresistible pull toward her and wondered if being a cad was really so horrible after all. Kissing her would be bad. And good too. Whether it was more bad than good he wasn't sure. He'd be breaking fraternisation rules and his own moral code. But fulfilling his fantasy of feeling her lips against his would be a goodness of colossal proportions. Too late he realised he'd been caught offside. His feelings had escaped their cage, run wild on his face for a moment too long and given him away. He saw the knowing in Annie's eyes and immediately he straightened his back and yanked his feelings back into place.

Then like a slate being wiped clean, Annie's penetrating gaze was gone, replaced with a politely pleasant look that somehow bothered him more than the look of complete knowing that had lit her eyes mere seconds before.

Chapter 5
18th December, 1941

"So?" Frank asked as he shook cigar ash into the wooden ashtray next to his desk.

"She's quick. Calm. Hard-working. I should be able to finish her training ahead of schedule."

"How far ahead?" Frank asked gruffly as he uncorked the decanter and poured himself some wine. Alex raised an eyebrow. Frank always had only one glass on the serving tray on his desk. It struck Alex as a sign that Frank had clear delineations in his head about who he felt was worthy enough to share a drink with him.

Alex had known this question was coming and schooled his features accordingly. He remarked with a neutral tone, "If she does well with weapons and ciphers, maybe the first week in January." Truth was he had no doubt they could finish by the end of December. His hope was that he could take the first week of January to get to know her better and that Annie would be open to the idea. If she didn't then at least he'd have a week to try to pull himself together after Annie broke his heart.

Frank huffed, his eyes narrowing. "That's when we want to put her in place. The Germans had time to rethink things since the Americans put their hat in the ring. They're expanding their *unterboot* reach across the Atlantic."

Alex looked up sharply. "U-boats? In the Caribbean too?"

"Yes. The region's got oil refineries, major shipping ports, aluminium and a healthy dose of the moneyed hoity-toities who fled to the tropical colonies when the Blitz started."

Alex exhaled sharply and rubbed his chin, his thoughts automatically going to his mother. And Annie. He stopped himself from clenching his jaw and looked directly at Frank who was watching him a tad too closely.

"Operation Drumbeat," Frank said with a sour shake of his head. "No doubt they're hoping for another 'Happy Time' as they call it: from mid '40 to a few months ago they were sinking eight merchant ships a month. We know our defences against their U-boats aren't great so we've got to move people in place quickly."

It was true. The Germans had the Allied Forces on the back-foot. Alex had seen the effects of the Blitz with his own eyes: bombed out buildings, looting, overflowing shelters, theft, fights. Lean times brought out the very worst in people. The U-boats did to ships what the bomber airplanes did to buildings. They wreaked havoc, caused even more scarcity and ratcheted up human suffering.

"So…" Frank said with a pert tap of his desk as he kept his eyes on Alex. "…fast track her training so we can get her out of your hair and into service. The minute she's ready for duty, report to me."

Alex nodded, his training kicking in as he steadied his nerves and kept his face impassive. He nodded and said, "Will do."

Chapter 6

23rd December, 1941

It had been ten days. All of them long and grueling, none of them having anything to do with new typewriting technology. Alex taught Annie to identify different types of weapons, the intricacies of knife-wielding and how to determine if she was being followed. He showed her how to pay greater attention to her surroundings, and how to use whatever was at hand to disarm an attacker. Alex gave her pages and pages of ciphers and codes to memorise for both the Allied and Axis forces, pages which she had to sit there and look at and couldn't remove from the building. Annie's feet ached from standing in her good shoes all day. Many nights she didn't crawl into bed until the moon hung high in the sky. Eventually Ma unpinned her lips and asked what sort of job she was really doing that she needed to be out so late. But all of that was tolerable in comparison to the wildly intense attraction she had to Alex.

She caught herself watching the movement of his lips, the ripple of his defined arms, wondering if his skin was as silky as it looked. Their conversations drifted into territory that while not inappropriate, bordered on friendly terms. It was just the two of them alone in the building all day every day, eating together and pondering life's vagaries between training sessions.

Yesterday, Annie breathed a sigh of relief when he'd told her they'd need to get an earlier start than usual since they would be outdoors. She felt like they were living in a sparsely furnished snow globe and hoped that being out in the real world would help to break the spell they were under. As they left that evening he told her to dress comfortably. "Trousers if you have them," he suggested. The mere thought of Ernesta Eudine Jones' face at the sight of her first daughter leaving the house in a pair of trousers made her chest tighten. Annie cleared her throat and said, "I don't."

The next day as dawn broke, Alex drove them to a freshly cut field deep in the country to practise shooting. Annie wasn't sure how inept he assumed she'd be that they needed such a deserted location, but she enjoyed the drive. No talk of spying or war. Just chitchat about fun childhood memories, a mutual fondness for the same books and food. Almost like they were courting. Annie sighed with contentment as she looked through the window, watching small chattel villages nestled among lush cane fields zip by, knowing she was in trouble.

She'd had a job before. The chemist, Mr. Fogarty, was a strange little man who reminded her of a patchwork quilt. His skin wrinkled until it puckered and was covered in patchy pink age spots. A head so bald that it was shiny. And chronic eczema that he was forever slathering with his own special ointments. Annie had dreaded going to work. Between his frequent attempts to look down her blouse and threats to cut her pay because she refused his advances, Annie wasn't particularly enthused by that job.

Now? Every day was something new, something she'd never thought about or done before that challenged her and made her feel like she was capable of much more than she'd ever dreamed. Her plans to migrate to Switzerland seemed even more plausible since she'd started training. At first the thought was big, untouchable and so very frightening. Now it felt like the next logical adventure. That's the thing with facing the unknown; the obstacles are impossible until you realise it's all in your head. She couldn't deny that much of her newfound faith and courage came from Alex's encouragement.

He didn't chastise. He gave advice. He didn't belittle. He encouraged. Alex had a knack for gently pointing out that Annie had already overcome so many obstacles and this challenge, the seemingly insurmountable task in front of her, was just one more to master.

The things Alex said didn't enter her ears like regular words did. They vibrated inside her, echoing as though they originated from a place long gone but never forgotten. What she felt for this man went beyond lust and infatuation. Everything about him rang with certainty. *He knows me and I know him,* she'd thought more than once. Gran had curious theories on such things, some nonsensical to Annie in her youth but logical now that she'd grown and seen more of life.

"What?" Alex asked when she sighed as he pulled the car to a stop in the shade of a tamarind tree.

"I don't know...but it's different when we talk. It makes sense, you know? As though I don't have to explain myself the way I do with other people." Annie hated how she fumbled the words. She felt like a simpleton the teacher would put at the back of the class to keep them out of the way of the bright children lest they contaminate them.

But instead of staring at Annie like her brain was no more than a shallow vessel that grew hair, Alex's eyes softened and he said, "I feel it too."

Whatever Annie sensed deepened and before she could stop herself she asked, "Do you believe in reincarnation?"

"Anything is possible," he said with a thoughtful shrug. "Maybe that's what it is. This tether I sense between us feels like you're an anchor for everything around me. Not in a way to hold me back but to keep me steady when I'm adrift."

They were words Annie didn't know she needed to hear. Thoughts she didn't know she needed expressed to her at least once in this lifetime. This feeling was so rich and unrepentant that she wondered how she had lived without it.

"Yes," was all she said and she didn't worry that it wasn't enough.

In the middle of the field, Alex set up targets of varying sizes that he'd taken out of his trunk along with a small pail. Annie looked at it questioningly. "For the shells," he explained. "We're meant to be spies so being incognito is a way of life. Remember that. No holes in trees, no bullet casings to say we were here. Plus we can melt them down and use them for other things. Can't waste materials during wartime."

Most of the day had gone when it happened. By that time, the sun was setting. Maybe she was overthinking it or maybe subconsciously she wanted to impress Alex. There was a lot to remember: stance, grip, angles, how to insert the bullets, not too much pressure when squeezing the trigger and all the rest of it. She had just finished loading the gun when she lost her hold and dropped it on her toes. She was too slow in stepping back to avoid the impact and with a loud thunk it hit her shoe and landed in the thick grass. Every time she heard a similar sound after that her heart hammered as she remembered the fear that it would go off, possibly shooting herself. As soon as Annie cried out in pain, Alex was at her side, unloading and pocketing the gun, lifting her into the car and taking off her shoe in one fluid motion.

"Blimey…that doesn't look fun," he said, dropping to one knee as they watched her toes swell to twice the size right before their eyes. "Well, I guess we can learn about first aid while we're here." He peered at her foot, trying to see it through the gauzy haze of her stocking. "In situations where there's no ice, heat or medicine, we try to get blood flowing to the area as quickly as possible to minimise pain and swelling."

Alex's hands twitched and then froze on Annie's ankle. He took a breath and then looked up, his eyes locking on hers. "I'll…" Alex cleared his throat. "…need to remove your nylons. May I?"

Annie had pictured some variance of this in her head for days. But him on one knee in an open sunlit field poised to take off her stockings had a warmly chivalrous feeling to it that she hadn't the mental dexterity to conjure. Her toes throbbed in time with her heart, both of them fit to burst. His hands were warm on her skin, his eyes willing her to say yes.

Time held its breath for Annie, as though certain her answer could shift the future either left or right. She felt the weight of its impatience in the golden light of the setting sun reflected in Alex's eyes. Saw it in the gilded dust motes suspended in the air. Heard it in the muted birdsong that was barely louder than the beating of her heart. And Annie knew that this was what she'd been waiting for all along.

"Yes," she said softly. The world heaved a sigh and regained its frenetic pace, grateful that she had restored its natural order.

Alex's eyes never left hers as his hands disappeared just beneath the hem of her dress, found the top of her stocking and slowly rolled it down until it fell in the grass. "I'll rub them a bit to get the blood flowing so it doesn't bruise as much, but it might hurt a little," Alex cautioned. Annie grimaced in pain, hands braced on the car seat as he started a slow and gentle massage.

"So...how did I do?" she asked between clenched teeth, desperate to inject some normalcy into the situation.

"Your aim is good and so is your stance. You're a natural at it, if I'm honest." His face lit up with a mischievous grin. "Your weapon handling could use some work though."

Annie laughed. "I knew you'd say that."

"Did you? How?"

"Yes," Annie answered with a coy smile. "Maybe my photographic memory has a built-in telegraphic feature too."

The mirth left his voice, turning husky as his gaze grew serious again. "What am I thinking now?"

He wants the same thing I do.

Ma warned me about men like him, Annie realised with a start. Men who smile too sweetly, are too smart, too devilishly handsome to let your guard down around.

But Ma is a fool. Because if she could feel the way Annie's blood was singing in her veins as it barrelled towards her feminine wiles, she would know that there is glory in a danger this sweet.

"You're wondering what *I'm* thinking."

His nod was almost imperceptible. "I am. Because we're on the same page about so many things and I hope that's the case right now."

He wants…no, needs to know I'm okay with what comes next. And I want that too.

In the end there were no words. Only the touch of their lips, the caress of their tongues and an end to weeks of their collective yearning.

Chapter 7
Christmas Eve, 1941

It rained during the night. Softly, slowly as though bathing the world with languid ease in feathery droplets. The sunlight was soft, golden as it crept across the floor of Alex's room with languid indifference. The white gossamer drape of the mosquito net cascaded from the ceiling and flowed over the bed, covering them and putting Annie in mind of two caterpillars wrapped in the same cocoon. Their bodies were intertwined, all of their previously unsaid words laid bare in every touch, shudder and sigh as the wee hours waned. Annie was not new to a man's pleasure but what she'd seen and felt with him during the night had eclipsed anything she'd known in the past.

Alex kissed the top of her head, his arms warm on her back and waist. "How's your foot, straight-shooter?"

Annie scowled, her lips pursed in mock indignation as she looked up at him and said, "It's been better. Although, knowing you, that's probably going to end up in my report."

"I pride myself on precision."

She smacked his chest and laugh.

"But honestly, I'm impressed with your professionalism and accuracy so far. Whoever suggested you to the boys in charge made a good choice. We'll finish your training next week and then you'll have the honour of choosing your code name."

Annie raised herself up on her arms and turned to Alex. "Really?" she beamed. "Can it be anything?"

"Well…they've made us stick to regional birds to make it easier to determine a spy's origin. They lump the whole Caribbean together, so you can choose birds from Cayman even," he said, reaching over to pick up his watch from the bedside table.

"Why birds?"

"They call spies bird watchers," he replied. He twisted his mouth into a sarcastic pucker. "The Brits aren't known for complicating things."

"Hmm." Annie's grandmother believed names held the great power and had named all of her grandchildren. Grace, she said, was going to be a vessel of faith and charity, the glue that held her family together. Wilbert was meant to be a genius to hear her tell it, but that didn't work out the way she had hoped. So far he was only smart enough to avoid prison, but maybe that did qualify him as a genius. She named Annie after the Russian grand duchess whom she believed was still alive. "A star girl like you goin' need a solid name. I look 'pon you face from the time you mother born you on that bed and say 'this child got a smart face… and a rude mouth'," she used to tell Annie. So for Annie, picking a name — her own name at that — was no small feat.

"What names are left?"

Alex shrugged as he kissed Annie again and untangled himself from the bedsheets so he could pull on his pants. "Haven't seen the list since I picked my own name. I'll have to get you an updated copy."

A smile lit Annie's face. "So what's *your* name?"

Alex grinned. "I chose the Antillean nighthawk, but I go by Nighthawk for short."

"Why that bird?"

"They're good at camouflage and are notorious for making loud booming noises." He winked. "One of my specialties is explosives."

Silently, Annie agreed.

Something crossed Alex's face and he took a deep breath as he sat next to her on the bed. "We probably should have talked about this before but the cat's out of the bag now."

Annie swallowed, her throat growing tight. "What?"

"I need to know…how much does being a career army woman mean to you?"

Annie bit her lip. "To be honest...not much, but don't tell them that if it means they'll kick me out."

Alex laughed, his shoulders relaxing a bit as he said, "No, no. Not like that. You see...I'm violating the ministry's no-fraternisation policy by being involved with you. We both are but I'm in more trouble because I'm senior and you haven't completed your training yet."

"What's the punishment?"

"Everything: forfeiture of pay, court marshall, possibly confinement which is a fancy word for military prison."

Annie's face fell. "Oh...so they're serious."

"Very."

"Right now a job is a job," she shrugged. She looked at him hopefully. "Truth is that I really want to move to Switzerland. Maybe open a little bakery on the side of an alp somewhere. A fresh start with more opportunities, less war, different weather...you know: change."

"I'm glad to hear that," he admitted ruefully. "I want to stay in the army, get some medals, help win the war… and truth be told I don't want my wife crouching in a foxhole somewhere."

They both started as the words left his mouth.

"I'm sorry, I shouldn't assume —"

"I didn't know you felt —"

They held their breath, eyes locked on each other as they reached out and clasped hands.

Alex brushed her cheek with his fingertips and murmured, "It feels like the next step. For me, at least. But I shouldn't assume it's the same for you."

"It is," Annie said with a shy smile.

He kissed her on the lips and said with a grin, "Looking forward to it."

Reluctantly, Alex stood and held out his hand to her. "Ready to get back to training?"

Blackouts made it difficult to get the full measure of the place Alex lived in since they'd arrived when it was pitch black and had starting pulling each other's clothes off from the time he unlocked the door. Light wasn't necessary for the kind of love-making they'd engaged in the night before. Now, Annie could see that Alex was quite well off. He'd explained that the one bedroom building he lived in had once been a stable located downwind of his parents' house. Only rich people could afford to convert an old stable into a bachelor lodging for their son. It was minimalist but warm, just like him. Annie liked it very much.

As they got dressed together a comfort crept over her that made her wish it could become a daily ritual. Wished they could have existed in a different time and met under other circumstances. *Granny was right*, Annie thought miserably. *Life isn't fair.*

Chapter 8

The island was shaking off the misery of war to embrace the holiday season. As they drove back to Humpton Street after an early morning shooting lesson, they passed men painting houses and women walking in packs toward Bridgetown with empty shopping bags. The lines at the ration office stretched further than usual and stores did a brisk trade as people bought whatever they could eke out of their coupons. Christmas was sacrosanct in Barbados, governed by traditions so tightly interwoven with religion that the slightest variance made your neighbours question your faith and sometimes even your sanity.

"Have you thought about your code name?"

"Hm? Maybe Heron. Or Pelican. But herons are better looking so probably that."

Alex looked over to see why Annie was distracted and slowed the car when he noticed her looking wistfully at the dresses in the department store window. "Trying to find your dress for Christmas morning?" he asked with a smile.

"What? Oh…" Annie smiled nervously and shook her head. "We make our own Christmas dresses. Or rather my sister, Grace, does since she's the one who stays at home these days."

"I would have thought you'd have an extra special dress since it's also your birthday."

Annie turned to him, brows pressed together in surprise. "I didn't mention…" Her face lit up and she threw her head back with a hearty laugh. "I forgot that my life story is tucked away in your files." She shook her head ruefully, pin curls bobbing against her shoulders. "There isn't much fanfare at home. Maybe a few extra cents on a combination Christmas-slash-birthday gift: like the pretty fan with a bit of lace trim that Ma and Grace made a few years ago. Last year I got a nice soap that smelled so luxurious and the bubbles were like satin on my skin," Annie said with a roll of her eyes.

Alex chuckled as he parked at the Humpton Street office. He looked through the windshield, his eyes distant for a moment before he turned to Annie.

"What would you want for your birthday if you could have anything at all in the world?"

Annie twisted her mouth and took a deep breath as she racked her brain. "You know, it's funny...since my birthday is on Christmas Day I don't think I ever separated it as being its own celebration. I always thought it was enough to have ham and baked goods." Annie turned to him, her eyes alight with curiosity. "What's Christmas like in England? Is snow soft? And is it really very white or just regular white?"

"It's cold as shite, that's for sure."

Annie laughed and then sighed. "I'd love to see it. Yes, it would be cold, but it would be worth it just to see the world asleep under all of that snow."

"There is a magic to it," Alex admitted. "Probably more so now that the war is on, oddly enough. Stores put up decorations — mostly old ones from last year. People scrimp and save their coupons and bits of money for that one gift that will make up for all the bombing and rationing that happened the other three hundred and sixty-four days. Word is that the Nazis won't be blitzing on Christmas. I'm not sure if it's to give them or us a break, but it doesn't matter. Because that's the one day in all of this turmoil that doesn't meld into the others, the one day that there's meant to be peace."

Annie smiled. "And hope."

Alex smiled too. "Yes. And hope."

***

His face softened as he watched her eyes shining. She talked of books she'd read with vivid descriptions of snow-laden trees, wind-whipped toboggan rides, warm cider and crackling fires in a hearth. But all Alex could think about was that it wasn't his intention to bed her so soon. He'd hoped he could have held out until after he'd finished her training. Mostly because the people they worked for knew everything about everyone and Alex didn't want them to ever question Annie's capabilities. It was something she didn't need, especially in this profession. That's why he'd coaxed her out of bed early so they could leave before his parents or anyone else came sniffing about.

Her training was almost complete. Annie needed to be put in place as soon as possible from what Frank said, even though Alex wasn't entirely sure what or where her assignment was. He caught himself hoping it wouldn't be dangerous. And that they didn't send him back to England. Or anywhere else for that matter. Alex hadn't cared before because he thought it was exciting to have a job that could take him anywhere in the world. Now his only thought was, *I want to stay here.*

His throat tightened, his palms sweated and a cold discomfort crawled through his chest. Annie was more to him than a warm body, more than a woman he hoped to while away the war with just because she was nearby. His feelings for Annie were real and, as she giggled about setting her sister's Christmas dress on fire last year, Alex realised just how much he loved her.

It was a daunting realisation but one that felt good to recognise. To lean into the emotion that eclipsed everything and made him want to be a better man for her.

"Do you like Christmas too?" he heard her ask.

He dragged his thoughts away from his emotions and replied, "I do."

Alex tapped the steering wheel for a moment, then glanced skyward at the thick clouds forming overhead. "It's going to rain."

Annie leaned forward and pursed her lips as she looked at the building. "There's mail sticking out of the louvre."

Of course, he thought to himself. It wasn't mail, but a blank sheet of paper that only meant one thing.

"Do you mind terribly if we end early? And perhaps I can take you home so you don't get caught in the rain again."

"Yes, thank you very much," she smiled.

***

Annie's house was tucked away at the end of a little lane in a modest village on the outskirts of Bridgetown. Christmas hung in the air, evidenced by the scent of fresh paint, clean laundry flapping noisily on every available clothesline and the aroma of ham and cake that wafted through the car windows.

Every head turned in their direction as the car trundled down the road, all of them waving in surprise to Annie as she waved back. Straight ahead, standing in front of a white house with windows trimmed in grey stood a woman holding a dish towel who was undoubtedly Annie's mother. Alex knew it was her not just from the same skin tone and striking good looks but because she was the only person in the lane with her hands akimbo waiting for the car to stop.

Annie's demeanour changed from the time her foot touched the ground. "Evening, Ma. This is

Mr Alexander James. He's the supervisor for my new typist job."

Alex took off his hat, smiled and held out his hand. "Evening, Mrs Jones."

"Mr James," she replied stiffly, swinging her dish towel onto her shoulder.

"It's a pleasure. Your daughter is a credit to your family. Very bright and capable."

"That's my Annie," Mrs. Jones said, her armour cracking a little as pride brought a reluctant grin to her face. "Annie, go help Gracie with the pudding."

Face fallen, Annie glanced at Alex over her shoulder as she walked slower than necessary to go inside.

"Now, Mr James. Tell me why you're really here. 'Cause I ain't raise my daughters to be no supervisor's tickling board. And these unusual hours she's working ain't normal secretarial time, war or not."

"That's correct, ma'am. A man knows to present himself when his intentions are more than platonic. Your daughter isn't just a friend anymore. It's my hope to court her — with your permission, of course."

"Hmph." She pouted her mouth the way only a Caribbean mother can when she's turning something over in her head. For the first time she looked Alex up and down, taking in the shine of his shoes, the knot of his necktie and then finally the gleam of the car behind him. Imperceptibly at first, she nodded.

"Alright," she said. She smiled. "You want some sorrel? It draw down real good," she added, making him almost falter in his resolve to leave.

"Actually ma'am, I'm hoping to get to town to find something for Annie's birthday before the stores close."

"Ah. Okay," she nodded, both impressed and surprised by his response. Alex extended his hand to her again, and this time she accepted it.

"I know it's unusual to ask this but Annie's birthday falls on Christmas which I know is normally a family day. Do you think I could come and visit her tomorrow?"

"After church though," she said. Alex grinned. No right-thinking Barbadian man would dare show up at this lady's house until church service had concluded.

Alex nodded and made his way back to the car. No sooner than he opened the door a thought crossed his mind. It was a thought that would take time and effort to pull off and Alex would need her mother's permission, but he knew it would be worth it.

Mrs Jones had just turned to walk back into the house. Just past her, Alex saw Annie and her siblings scrambling to get away from the window lest their mother catch them eavesdropping.

"Excuse me," Alex said to get her attention as he walked toward her. She turned to him, her eyebrows raised in question.

"I wanted to do something special for Annie. If you don't mind me asking…how long will you be at church?"

Chapter 9

Bridgetown was deserted by the time Alex parked the car in front of the Spice House. Bounding up the stairs two at a time, he arrived at the landing and had barely raised his hand to knock when he heard the gruff voice telling him to come in.

Frank's face was ruddy as though he'd gotten into the brandy prematurely. He scowled, pissed off that he had to curtail his Christmas drinking to deal with Alex. Frank squinted at Alex and got right to the point. "Did you fuck her?"

"No."

"Then why was she at your house all night?"

"She was injured during training yesterday."

The glass in Frank's hand trembled, his thinly veiled rage seeping out of him as he tried to rein it in. "Unless she was harpooned with a

German spear that we need to examine, you can take her to the hospital like a regular civilian."

Alex looked down at the floor. "Which she technically still is at this point."

"Don't anger me, boy," Frank hissed through clenched teeth. "You knowingly flouted the only rule I gave you."

"I said I didn't have relations with her," Alex repeated, his face growing stony. "My priority is training her and helping our side win the war."

"Hmph." Frank downed half the liquor in one shot and said, "Keep it that way."

"But, out of curiosity…" Alex began. "If things did escalate and we wanted to get married, it would be fine if one of us left service, correct?"

Frank glared at him.

"Hypothetically, of course," Alex said with an easy tilt of his head.

"I don't like theories. They make me uncomfortable. I like facts — cold and indisputable nuggets of truth that bear up to scrutiny."

"It's a legitimate question from your subordinate who doesn't want to run afoul of the rules," Alex said with a straight face.

Frank squeezed the glass, his knuckles turning white. "Then, yes…it wouldn't pose a problem.

Alex kept back a smile. "Thanks for the clarity. If there's nothing else, may I be dismissed?"

"I'm warning you: stay on my good side. If I ever catch you on the wrong end of it, you won't like it."

"Yes, sir."

Chapter 10

Christmas Day, 1941

"Annie, Gracie, Bertie, I ain't calling wunna again!" Ma shouted angrily as she stuffed a handful of mints inside her handbag. Ma hated two things in equal measure: tardiness and being short-paid. Her dander was all the way up that morning, especially since she was set to sing the Christmas solo for the first time, an honour she had finally wrestled away from Bessie Carmichael. She'd put on some lipstick and her hair was extra nice, pressed straighter than a derby horse's mane. Annie was buttoning Grace's dress and Wilbert was packing his ration books into a neat stack at the bottom of the wardrobe. Less than a minute later the foursome was headed to church in the weak pre-dawn light.

The house smelled of ham, jug-jug and Ma's special Christmas pone recipe. Ma claimed it only had grated cassava, sugar, coconut and spices but Annie firmly believed there was something else to it because no-one else's pone tasted like hers. It was the first day in a while that Annie had seen her family so early and it was nice to be with them on Christmas. By five o'clock that morning, they had crowded around her at the dining room table, singing happy birthday and offering her their gifts. Ma and Grace made her the most stunning hair ornament: a fashionable flower to pin into her hair that looked very chic with her church dress. Wilbert gave her a ration book. Annie thanked him and stuffed it under the floor boards.

Church was everything they expected it to be: Ma was the perfect Christian diva, putting the soul in solo and bringing a tear to even Bessie Carmichael's eyes as she belted out God Rest Ye Merry Gentlemen. With warm cheeks and bright eyes, she returned to their pew and Annie couldn't help but wonder why she'd never noticed how glorious a singer she was. The whole church had applauded like they were at a Billie Holiday concert. *Miss Holiday is an excellent singer but Ma could take her*, Annie thought. The pride that welled up in her was unlike anything she'd felt for Ma before. She leaned over as the pastor headed back to the pulpit and said, "You got all of those singers covered down, Ma." She turned to Annie, her proud smile faltering for a second before a tear slipped out of her eye and said, "Thanks, baby." She dropped a wet kiss on Annie's forehead and hugged her tight. Christmas felt just as warm and sweet as it ever did.

The sun was bright overhead and hummingbirds flitted through the tangle of plants that dotted the church grounds as the congregation spilled out after the service. Most of the church-goers lived in the adjoining villages so most of them walked together. They sang the hymns again, louder this time and a bit out of key as everyone joined in. Ida Bradshaw and Maisie Watson shouted, "Do the solo again! Do it again!" to Ma who feigned embarrassment until the demands of her adoring public got to her and she did her encore as they turned onto the lane.

Annie was in the middle of the crowd so she was still singing when the group stopped walking without warning. She bumped into Miss Watson by accident as a low murmur hummed through the crowd. "What?" Annie asked Gracie who was holding her hand. Gracie shrugged and said, "Let's see." Both of them pushed to the front and right there before them was the most beautiful thing they'd ever seen. Gracie clutched her hand tighter and gasped, "It's a white Christmas, Annie." Their little chattel house that they left like normal that morning was now surrounded by a layer of small bright white grits of crushed marl that almost glowed in the bright Barbadian sunlight. Tears formed in Annie's eyes as she took everything in. Ma was all smiles as she came to stand next to her daughter. "You like it, Annie?"

"But Ma…how can we afford this? I thought we didn't have enough left after burying Gran."

"It's that fellow who dropped you home, Mister James. He wanted to do this for you and asked my permission yesterday."

Ma cocked her head to the side and said, "And that ain't all. He said he was bringing a birthday dress for you this evening, but act surprised when you get it." Ma puckered her mouth in approval. "Planning on courting you too."

Annie looked at Ma in amazement. "He told you so?"

"Yes, miss girl. Now, listen…" she said, face stern as she pushed her hands into her hips. "…he's a decent man so don't mess it up. Handsome too which means good-looking children. Normally you don't get all two together so if you ain't sure how to proceed with him, ask me and I would direct you."

Grace and Annie broke into a fit of giggles. Above all else, Ma was practical.

The neighbours were in awe of how ethereal their house looked, set on the layer of marl that surrounded it. Annie was so happy she could burst. Her house was beautiful, a new dress was on the way and Ma approved of the man she was falling in love with. She was even more excited to see Alex now.

***

A full moon hung in the sky, dusting silvery light on the shingled rooves as darkness fell and a hush covered the village. The bottom halves of windows were shuttered in case of rain. Doors were pulled in but not locked. Children crawled between their parents and siblings to go to sleep, dried khus-khus grass crackling beneath their little hands and feet.

Annie closed up the house entirely so she could read by the lantern without dreading the wail of the ARP Warden's siren. It was Annie's birthday gift to herself, that little bit of extra oil she was using. Reading during the day was harder now that she was training. And it lacked the cosy decadence that's part and parcel of reading before bedtime: the easy night-song of crickets and whistling frogs in the background as she turned every page, the gentle drift toward sleep as the story enveloped her.

She lit the lamp and sat in Gran's old rocking chair, her ears waiting for the waterfall of sounds. A crackle as the caned seat accepted her weight, a groan as the chair's joints expanded and contracted, a creak as the old floorboards sighed in protest. Annie had just removed the bit of ribbon from the place where she'd left off when she heard a gentle knock on the house.

She opened the door and there, glazed in moonlight, was Alex. Annie tilted her head and smiled at him, her heart filling with the sight of him.

He stood on the top step and reached out to take her in his arms. If she'd had doubts that she loved him before, they fell to the ground and shattered. They embraced and kissed all in one fluid motion as though they'd practiced the sequence a thousand times. His body was warm, firm on hers as he held her to him. His tongue was soft, intoxicating on hers as they kissed.

"Merry Christmas, sugar," he said.

"Thank you so much. I can't believe you did this for me. And all because you know I wanted to see snow," Annie said in disbelief as she held his face between her hands.

"Believe it," he said as he lifted Annie down from the step and led her to his car. "I didn't want to intrude on your family time, but I really wish I could have seen the look on your face. Plus my mother would have flayed me if I wasn't home this morning, so there's that," he said with a grin.

"It's so amazing," Annie said looking around the house. Even with just the moonlight, the marl seemed to glow all around them.

"But I wanted to get you something for just you for your birthday."

Annie turned to him, smiling. "Really?"

"Yes. This." Alex reached through the car window and brought out a long box. "It's a dress. Your mother was particular in telling me to make sure it's modest and that your favourite colour is yellow. I hope you like it. Happy birthday."

It was all Annie could do not to dissolve into tears in his arms. It was the first time that someone didn't treat her birthday like an afterthought. To be celebrated on her own was something she hadn't considered before. It made her rethink the things she'd accepted without question for so long. Alex made her feel seen. Not just the way he recognised her photographic memory or helped her see that she was capable of so much more than the rest of the world did. But because he listened and took the time to meet her where she was in life. Gran always said, "to be understood is to be loved" and Annie finally knew what she meant.

She put her arms around his neck and tiptoed to kiss him on the cheek. "I love you."

"Love you more, sugar."

Alex leaned forward and kissed her on the lips, a kiss so soft and sweet that Annie thought she couldn't wait to spend the rest of her Christmases with him.

**KEEP READING FOR AN EXCERPT FROM
BENEATH THE SUNLIT SEA,
THE FOLLOW-UP WORLD WAR II ROMANCE
NOVEL!**

BENEATH THE SUNLIT SEA
CHAPTER 1

The new job I pretend to do is simple. I'm stationed at the bay office, a quaint wooden hut on a beachside dock that juts out over pristine white sand in the turquoise Caribbean Sea. I handle cargo manifests and permits for passengers who traverse the colonies on the Lady Boats. An entire fleet of them dock at Carlson Bay: SS Lady Hawkins, SS Lady Nelson, SS Lady Drake, etcetera. The naming convention isn't particularly interesting, but I suspect that the imagined grandiosity helps the owners charge more to the deck passengers who are just making stops between here and the other islands. Now that the war is in full swing, it's hard to tell how much longer these Lady Boats will stay in service. Two years ago, the Lady Somers was turned into a war boat, swapping daybeds for warheads, and deployed to Europe. Last year, it was sunk off the Bay of Biscay. Since then two more converted ships were attacked by German U-boats intent on disrupting our supply chains: Lady Hawkins and Lady Nelson. The Lady Boats provide a critical lifeline. Yes, they ferry passengers from here to Halifax and back, but they also carry mail, food, weapons and cargo. Every time one is sunk, it throws a wrench in the machine that is war.

On the surface, I fill out permits, affixing my signature and a stamp to the slips, making sure the bearer's photograph matches their face. In reality, I'm here to observe suspicious travellers and make note of known enemy spies. It's the details I'm more interested in; misspellings or smudges on the pre-typed slip, telltale giveaways that would let me know it's a forgery. I've committed a few key faces and names to memories but new players could always pop up on the scene so I also observe attitudes and mannerisms.

It's harder than it sounds and more critical than I make it out to be. If it weren't for the persistent threat of danger, I'd find it quite boring. But then again I've always been attracted to danger even if I don't look it. The recruiting officer's voice dripped with sarcasm when he said I look like a librarian who inherited her wealthy aunt's spoon collection. I smirked in amusement at this assessment from a rotund man who seemed ill-suited to anything that involves stealth. I suspect that I was exactly what he wanted. Being pretty is an asset, I gather. The female spies are not meant to be incongruous. A pleasing face and bright smile are necessary diversions given the climate.

I'm neither rough hewn like a fish monger nor overly polished like London socialites, but I toe the line between the two, like a secretary to a powerful industrialist.

We're just past the summer rush. Ripened mangoes and cherries leach their scents into the air from bulky canvas bags. Heady parfums issue from a sturdy brown trunk being moved by a chubby stevedore. The dock teems with life, people from both high and low stations wearing suits and dresses eked out of rationed cloth. The plantocracy is returning from visiting relatives in the other colonies. The poor have scraped together one-way passage to find work in similarly depressed economies, telling themselves that suffering in a new locale may be the morale boost they need. The conservative ones look scandalised as they give a wide berth to two women coming down the gangplank chatting gayly in blouses and boxy trousers. Four years ago, a woman was jailed in Los Angeles for wearing pants to court. I quirk my eyebrow. It seems that everyone hasn't caught on to the real travesty of war; that women are being forced to do men's work and simultaneously refusing to stay in their place.

Whatever that meant.

I straighten the hummingbird brooch on my lapel and go back to updating my booking records, a task I've learned to do while (surreptitiously) keeping an eye on the people hurrying past my little desk. There's an art to picking out who's most likely to be gathering intelligence. They probably won't be in large groups so that cuts today's possibilities in half. Even if they're solo, they won't have big trunks — the less they can leave behind at a moment's notice, the better. If they're from outside of the Caribbean, they tend to be taken in by the brown pelicans swooping overhead, the white sandy beach, the undulating liquid topaz of the ocean. Regional travellers often hurry down the gangway, eager to reach their inn or cousin's house so they can offload their heavy bags and take a piss. No, a spy's eyes will flit back and forth, silently count the staff, take note of entrances and observe the patrols.

Lucille, the old woman with the hairy mole who trained me for the official non-threatening part of the job, is looking forward to retirement so she can get away from the bay. She's a frisky old thing, indifferent to women and attentive to the men who sidle up to the booth. She often prays that it's the Lord or a particularly randy soldier that takes her in her sleep and not bombs dropping in the middle of the night. These days her fears are justified, even here beneath swaying palm trees. Hints of turmoil are everywhere. Merchant ships carrying flour and canned goods now have guns on their sterns to defend against air and submarine attacks. Torpedo boats were sent from Trinidad to patrol these waters and even the harbour authorities now have depth charges and mounted guns on their small boats.

Overhead, the pelicans are restless, gullets wobbling with silvery fish and sea water as they scurry back to their little island just up the coast. On bright, clear days, Pelican Island looks like it's breathing, humming with the to and fro of the brown birds as they squawk about. I used to envy their freedom, the ability to fly away from danger, the chance to pack up and leave it all behind when a situation gets tremulous. But now even Pelican Island is under siege since it was commandeered as an internment camp for enemy aliens. During the war, no-one and nothing is safe.

My grandmother always said humans are the most useless species; we need tools and telegrams and stoves to survive. Ma-Ma, as we called her, had lived through enough to know better.

"Watch them animals," she always cautioned. "If ants ain't eat it, you don't touch it. If you see animals running, go behind them. Use the li'l bit of sense you got to follow them." Animals detect drops in air pressure, changes in wind direction and vibrations in the earth that alert them to threats. Her first born, my mother, recalled that as a child she had been enchanted when thousands upon thousands of dragonflies had suddenly descended on the island like a black cloud of winged fairies.

"Hmph," was all Ma-Ma had said as she rubbed flour from her hands and looked outside. She'd tutted miserably and went back to rolling dumplings for the soup, even though the hair on her arms stood on end for hours after that. When neighbouring St. Vincent's volcano erupted later, raining heaps of ash down on our island, my mother said my grandmother simply smacked her lips and said, "The dragonflies tell we so evuh since."

I haven't seen such things in my own lifetime, but watching those pelicans take flight with such fervour makes me anxious to get home.

***

And yet, if it's possible, my anxiety doubles in an instant. The last passengers hustle off the gangplank, the boards quivering beneath shiny brogues and leather peep-toes. Something in the way the last man on the gang plank shifts the trilby hat on his head and hefts the suitcase in his hand makes my stomach clench. I know that jaunty gait, that upright posture. I know those coffee-coloured eyes as they catch sight of me for the first time in six months.

My breath hitches in my chest as all of my training deserts me as this man who looks everything like a Hollywood movie star walks toward me with a wrinkled brow and a smile plastered on his face. He is like art, at its most beautiful when captured in vivid hues of blood and tears.

I never thought I'd see him again. A reasonable expectation since they'd told me he'd been killed along with half the crew when a torpedo hit his ship. But here he is without a scar. My curiosity mingles with relief, tussling inside me until all that marks my face is stunned confusion. How did he get here? Why was he still so achingly handsome? Why the hell didn't he write?

I'd loved him, of course. Loved him in a way that made my heart sing and my stomach sink all at once. I'd thought I'd known hardships; hunger, my father going off to war, my sister being forced into a job way beneath her intelligence. But none of those minor inconveniences compared to losing him. I wish I could say I had fielded the loss with countless dalliances until he'd become nothing more than a vaguely remembered name. I couldn't.

His name is Alex James and his eyes light up but then his shoulders tense when he catches the look on my face. He reaches the counter. He slides his permit over the mahogany surface and his hand lingers on the paper as the words, "Annie?" escape his lips as mere wisps of air.

I focus on the permit which alleges that his name is James Walker and he's come from New York to visit family.

It's all lies.

"Where were you?" I can barely squeeze the words out of my mouth, I'm so angry.

Alex hesitates, torn between pacifying me and sticking to the status quo before he whispers, "Meet me at our spot tonight at seven. You deserve an explanation."

"And you deserve nothing but ticks and famine," I say as I clench my pen in my fist. I glare at him. He has no idea what life has been like for me since his boat went down, no remorse about looking me in the face and asking me to forgive him for everything that's taken place since he chose another life over me.

His voice grows lower, more urgent as he sees Leonard and Albert two of the Harbour and

Bridge Police motioning to each other that the passenger has been at the booth for an inordinately long time. "The morning sun is brighter than the evening moon," he whispers hurriedly as Leonard walks over.

Instantly, I still my hand.

"Evenin', Annie. Everythin' good?" Leonard asks.

"I'm not sure," I reply as my eyes bore into Alex's brown ones. "Seems the gentleman has lost his way."

"Oh?" Leonard says as he takes a half step closer.

"Yes. Mr...*Walker* made a bit of an error. Seems he thought he could have made this journey unscathed..."

"*Ohh?*" Leonard's voice and eyebrows raise as one as he tightens his grip on the truncheon. The war has put everyone on edge, it's true, but the look in Leonard's eyes lets me know that his reasons for intervening are more personal than patriotic.

Alex's face softens something deep in my chest, transporting me back to nights spent with my head on his chest and days kissing his lips. My resolve deserts me and the paper trembles in my hand. Hurting him will only make it impossible for me to sleep tonight. The alternative, meeting him in the hopes of getting a proper explanation for why he left may finally give me the peace I've been seeking for months.

"It's fine," I say airily. I'm so worked up that I stamp the permit too hard making it slide across the permit and leaving a dark streak on my desk. My face feels like it's about to spasm as I both glare and smile at Alex when I hand the permit back to him. "The gentleman needs directions to the nearest bar. The rough sea really did him in."

Leonard's begrudgingly drops his hand and watches the passenger nod gratefully to me and stride off the pier without looking back. Leonard sidles up to the counter, his eyes aglow as he once again asks me to go to the dinner club with him. I envy him his confidence. Displaying a smile that is half gums, half teeth is beyond the scope of my courage.

"Tell the truth, Annie. A sexy thing like you, all hips and hair, gotta have a man overseas. That's why you ain't want me to keep you company?"

The problem with Leonard is he believes he's juicier than an overripe orange and he makes sure every woman within spitting distance knows it. Frankly, if I wanted to be covered in bodily fluids, I would have been a nurse instead of a spy. I bite my tongue to restrain myself and again, I refuse.

As I prepare to close up the shutters, I notice a tiny slip of paper on the counter where the man's permit was:

I'll send a car at six. Walk the rest of the way.
Destroy this.

Visit **www.calliebrowning.com** to sign up for author updates.

www.ingramcontent.com/pod-product-compliance
Lightning Source LLC
LaVergne TN
LVHW041617070526
838199LV00052B/3179